The Cursed Necklace

'The Cursed Necklace'
An original concept by Katie Dale
© Katie Dale

Illustrated by Lala Stellune

Published by MAVERICK ARTS PUBLISHING LTD

Studio 11, City Business Centre, 6 Brighton Road,

Horsham, West Sussex, RH13 5BB

© Maverick Arts Publishing Limited February 2021

+44 (0)1403 256941

A CIP catalogue record for this book is available at the British Library.

ISBN 978-1-84886-774-1

www.maverickbooks.co.uk

White

This book is rated as: White Band (Guided Reading)

The CURSED Necklace

By **Katie Dale**

Illustrated by **Lala Stellune**

Chapter 1

Akil and Neema lived in Ancient Egypt. One hot day, they went to fetch water from the River Nile with their dog, Pepi.

Suddenly, Pepi ran over to a nearby bush and started digging in the sand.

"What can you smell, boy?" Neema asked.

"It's probably a bone," Akil said.

"Or a smelly old sandal," Neema added, wrinkling her nose. But Pepi didn't dig up a bone or a smelly sandal. He dug up a leather pouch. "What's that?" Neema frowned.

They walked to the bush and sat down in the shade. Neema opened the pouch.

Inside was an intricate beaded necklace with falcon-shaped clasps. Neema and Akil gasped. They had never seen anything so beautiful!

"It looks very expensive!" Akil frowned. "I wonder why it was buried under a bush?"

"Maybe someone dropped it when they were resting in the shade?" Neema said. "It is very hot today."

"Probably," Akil agreed. "We should return it to its owner."

Neema nodded. "Let's go to the market and see if anyone is looking for a lost necklace." She slid the necklace back into its pouch.

Chapter 2

As they walked through the bustling market, Neema's mouth watered. The food smelled amazing.

"How many loaves of bread do you think we could get in exchange for our necklace?" Neema wondered hungrily.

Akil frowned. "It isn't our necklace to swap," he said.

"Finders keepers," Neema argued, pulling the necklace out of its pouch. "Whoever lost it is clearly rich anyway!"

"No!" Akil said, snatching the necklace. "It's not ours to trade! Besides, I saw it first!"

"No you didn't!" Neema cried, grabbing it.

"Hey!" a man shouted suddenly. "That's my necklace! You found it!"

A big hairy man pushed through the crowds towards them.

"I'm so glad we can return it to you!" Akil said, smiling. "Give it back to him, Neema."

But Neema frowned. The hairy man didn't look rich. Why would he have an expensive necklace?

"Where did you lose it?" Neema asked him.

"Beneath some bushes near the river," the man said, glowering. "By the sphinx."

"Oh... okay," Neema sighed. She passed him the necklace, but just then a guard walked by.

"Stop thief!" the guard cried suddenly, pointing at Neema's hands. "That's Tutankhamun's stolen necklace!"

Chapter 3

"What?" Neema gasped. "I didn't steal the necklace! I found it and was just returning it to its owner!" She pointed at the hairy man, but he had disappeared into the crowd.

"Oh really?" said the guard. "You were returning it to Tutankhamun's coffin in his tomb, were you?"

"What do you mean?" Neema asked, turning pale.

"They say anyone who steals from a tomb is cursed – and in your case it's true!" the guard said, grabbing the necklace. "I'm arresting you for tomb robbery!"

"But we didn't steal it!" Akil cried. "Our dog dug it up!"

"I don't believe you," the guard said. "You're both coming with me!" He tried to grab Neema and Akil, but Pepi jumped up and grabbed the necklace - and ran away! "Hey! Stop, thieves!" the guard yelled, as Akil and Neema ducked, dodged and disappeared into the crowds.

Akil, Neema and Pepi sprinted out of the market, along the river, and all the way home.

"We made it!" Neema puffed. "But we left our water behind!"

"Oh no!" Akil panted. "We can't go back – the guards will arrest us for tomb robbery!"

"But we didn't steal anything!" Neema sighed. "How can we prove we're innocent?"

"We can't," Akil said. "But we can give the necklace back to its owner. Maybe that will be enough."

Neema rolled her eyes. "Akil, that big hairy man is not the necklace's owner - he must have stolen it from Tutankhamun's tomb!"

"That's what I mean," Akil said. "We need to give the necklace back to its real owner - Tutankhamun."

Neema stared at him, wide-eyed. "You mean…"

Akil nodded gravely. "We need to put it back in Tutankhamun's tomb. Before anything else goes wrong."

Chapter 4

As Akil and Neema hurried to the tomb, their luck got worse and worse.

First, Neema trod on a snake, and almost got bitten. Then Akil almost walked straight into a guard. Then when they finally reached the tomb, they couldn't find the way in!

"This is hopeless!" Akil sighed, sinking down onto the hot sand.

"There must be an entrance somewhere,"
Neema frowned, looking around. "The big hairy
robber found a way in."

Suddenly, Pepi started digging behind a large
boulder.

"Oh no! I hope he's not digging up more
treasure!" Akil cried.

"I hope he is!" Neema said excitedly. "Maybe
Pepi can find a way in!"

Sure enough, as Pepi dug, the boulder rolled away slightly, revealing a hole in the ground.

"Look!" Neema cried. "It's a way into the tomb!"

Akil gulped as he stared at the long, dark staircase. "You first."

"No, you first!" Neema argued.

Suddenly Pepi scampered past them into the hole. "Woof! Woof!"

Neema and Akil looked at each other.

"We never usually argue this much," Akil said. "It must be the curse."

Neema nodded. "I can't wait for this to be over." She took Akil's hand. "Let's go down together."

"Together," Akil agreed.

Carefully, they lit a torch and made their way down the long dark tunnel.

Chapter 5

"Ouch!" Neema cried as she tripped on a rock. Her voice echoed creepily in the darkness, and dust rained down on them from the roof.

"Careful," Akil warned. "They say some tombs are booby-trapped."

"What?!" Neema squealed. "Then let's just drop the necklace, find Pepi, and get out of here!"

"No," Akil shook his head. "We have to put the necklace back on Tutankhamun's coffin."

As they walked on, torchlight flickered over golden animals, jewellery, statues, and baskets of food... but no coffin. Just then, they heard Pepi bark.

"Come on," Akil said. "The burial chamber must be just a bit further inside."

"I hope we don't get lost!" Neema whispered. As they edged their way through a doorway, they gasped. The chamber walls were covered in gold and decorated with hundreds of pictures. And there, in the middle of the room, was an enormous golden coffin.

"Woof!" Pepi barked at the coffin.

"I-is that... where Tutankhamun's b-body is?"
Neema whispered nervously.

Akil nodded. "I'll go and put the necklace back."
Neema's hands shook as she passed it to Akil.

"There," he said, replacing it. He sighed with
relief. "It's all over."

"Oh no it isn't," said a deep voice behind them.
It was the big hairy man!

Chapter 6

The big hairy man walked slowly towards them. Pepi barked. "Boo!" the man yelled back. Pepi whined and scampered past him out of the chamber. "Give me the necklace," the man demanded.

"No," Akil said. "You have to leave it here. It's cursed."

"Cursed? Ha!" the man laughed, snatching the necklace. "There's no such thing as curses.

The only bad luck I've had is you kids digging up the necklace from my hiding place after I stole it the first time!"

Suddenly, there was a loud rumble and a statue near the door fell over with an enormous **CRASH!** Everyone screamed.

"It's the curse!" Akil wailed.

"It's a booby-trap!" Neema squealed.

"No... it's a guard!" the hairy man cried.

Sure enough, everyone turned to see the guard - and Pepi!

"Woof! Woof!" Pepi barked.

The hairy man turned pale. Then he smiled. "Thank goodness you're here, guard!" he cried. "I followed these kids and found them trying to steal more treasure from the tomb!"

"That's not true!" Akil yelled.

"He's the robber, not us!" Neema insisted.

"You caught these kids with the necklace earlier in the market," the hairy man said, smiling. "You know they're the thieves, not me."

Akil and Neema looked at each other nervously. How could they make the guard believe them?

"You're coming with me," the guard said sternly. He stepped towards them.

Chapter 7

But instead of arresting Akil and Neema, the guard grabbed the big hairy man!

"You believe us?" Akil gasped.

"When I heard your dog barking and saw you go into the tomb, I followed you down here thinking I'd catch you stealing again," the guard explained. "But then I heard everything this man just said." He glared at the hairy man as he tied his hands together and led them all out of the tomb. "I now know that he stole the necklace and buried it, and you two accidentally dug it up and tried to return it to its owner," he continued. "You were telling the truth all along. I'm sorry I didn't believe you before."

"That's okay," Neema smiled. "I'm just glad you believe us now! And I'm glad to be out of that creepy tomb!"

"And I'm glad King Tutankhamun has finally got his necklace back," Akil grinned. "And no one's cursed anymore."

"Woof! Woof!" Pepi barked happily, digging in the sand.

"No, Pepi! Stop!" Neema and Akil cried. "Don't dig up more cursed treasure!" But Pepi kept digging and found...

...a smelly old sandal!

"Oh Pepi!" everyone laughed.

The End

Book Bands for Guided Reading

The Institute of Education book banding system is a scale of colours that reflects the various levels of reading difficulty. The bands are assigned by taking into account the content, the language style, the layout and phonics. Word, phrase and sentence level work is also taken into consideration.

Maverick Early Readers are a bright, attractive range of books covering the pink to white bands. All of these books have been book banded for guided reading to the industry standard and edited by a leading educational consultant.

Pink
Red
Yellow
Blue
Green
Orange
Turquoise
Purple
Gold
White

To view the whole Maverick Readers scheme, visit our website at www.maverickearlyreaders.com

Or scan the QR code above to view our scheme instantly!